THE CURSE OF SABRINA DEBOIS

Sylvester Murray

The Curse of Sabrina Debois

Printed in the United States of America

This is a work of fiction. Names, characters, place, and incidents either are the product of the author's imagination or used fictitiously. Any resemblance to actual events or locales or persons, living or dead, is entirely coincidental.

Table of Contents

CHAPTER 1

It has been known for many years that a healer is an essential part of any community; an army needs a healer in order to succeed. A healer knows about healthy life habits and keeps in tune with their environment. Superstition follows a healer wherever they go; they are intertwined with voodoo practices. There is no one way to be involved in voodoo or healing; each country has different methods, according to their environmental changes.

In a small village in Haiti, there was once an unquestioning belief that healing and voodoo was the only life to accept. Natural disasters are natural to this country, so natural healings would also be. In this village, it is believed that the soul of the old healer is halved and travels and is then reborn with the new healer, their soul develops, and gradually the old healer would start to die, and more of their soul would be reborn in that of the new one. Many people fear their healers, as any skill that they picked up would be passed on to the next healer regardless of, if it were good or bad. It is believed that the Iwa calls upon the new healer and he decides to listen to the Iwa's call. However, if the individual were to refuse, then misfortune would fall upon them.

Sabrina Debois is the best-known healer of them all. She could heal those close to death and help people with year-long ailments. She grew up in a small village in Haiti, where rituals and spirits roamed free. All manners of different beliefs were intertwined and reborn through thousands of years of development. From her death, the country has been cursed and ravaged by nature. The village in which she lived is now barren, their homes flattened in a terrible cyclone and the entire town decimated. Her grave is the only main thing left in the city. It is surrounded by all shades of green nature, confetti with flowers and vines. It is known that her spirit roams around, protecting her ancestors from meeting the same fate she did. She grew up in a small hut on the side of her village, with her parents and siblings.

'You shined like the sun when you were born' her mother would smile and reminisce.

Her mother knew she was destined to be a healer, learning to read and write at a very young age; she knew that there was something important about her child.

And she was right; her talent seemed to grow and develop every day, her natural interest in making people better peaked the attention of family members and friends.

Until one day, a terrible flood hit their village in Haiti, showers of water belly flopped onto the town, ripping away any standing buildings that came in its path. Trees were ripped from their roots, and the violent rush of cold brown water drowned out the screams of people. Sabrina's older sister happened to be caught in the main pull of the flood while walking into the market. Her body looked like a wet piece of paper, limp and fragile. She seemed barely alive. Healers from across the island came to the village, healing rituals and ceremonies to appease the Iwa were performed. The echo of the drums ran throughout the village, and the scent of rum that had been poured on the ground wafted into the noses of everyone in the village. Many healers came to the Debois's residence, almost bankrupting the family. All saying the same thing

'She is close to death; there's nothing we can do for her.'

They made different recommendations of methods to make her comfortable; watch for her soul at night, don't eat the tops of watermelons or grapefruits or she will die.

Sabrina's parents had lost hope; the funeral would have to be small as so many people were unwell and injured. They couldn't tempt fate. Sabrina heard her mother weeping luxuriously to herself one night after their home had been remade, she had an idea to help her sister and to stop her mother's tears. She went into her sister's room and moved each bone until they were straight. She fixed them with any sticks she could find to help them stay in place. Sabrina's mother saw her shuffling around the house and going to her sister, thinking that she wanted to help and smiling to herself.

'My little healer is doing her work.'

2

Until a few days later, Sabrina's sister's fever broke. You were no longer aware of her breathing as it was relaxed. A kind of breathing everyone takes for granted until we can no longer hear our loved ones doing it. The family was so ecstatic that she was okay, that they ignored everything pointing to any evidence that Sabrina helped. Except for her mother, and after a while, it was clear that Sabrina had helped.

As Sabrina grew up, it became more apparent to those around her that she was no ordinary child. While her cousins and siblings played together and helped with the family; Sabrina was collecting plants and ingredients to make ointments and supplements to heal herself as well as her friends and family. Sabrina's mother always boasted about her daughter's penmanship and her closeness with the Iwa when the family went to the Ounfo.

'The Iwa smiles on her when she enters the room, you can feel their presence when she is around' Sabrina's mother would smile as she praised all her children; it was always clear who was her favorite child. The way her voice raised with pride as she spoke about Sabrina was evident and the small glint of light that shone from her eyes whenever she was mentioned.

For this reason, Sabrina never really got along with her siblings. Her brothers would tease her for having very little friends, and her sisters would laugh at her when she would go on walks in the hope of finding new items to add to her collection. After a while, it became clear to people that Sabrina was gifted. She would sit with her elderly grandparents who would complain about pain in their back, and not long after her visit; the pain had gone. It was not until her twelfth birthday that anyone started to realize her potential truly.

The village healer had entered the village to help a young girl with fever when he saw Sabrina. He sensed a part of himself in her; he could feel his own interest in the healing powers that he had as a young boy, now in her. He walked up to the young girl.

'Sabrina Debois' he said without introduction.

'I would like you to help me' he chanted holding a hand out for her to take.

The people surrounding her stared wide-eyed they looked at each other and frowned, mumbling questions to themselves about what was happening.

They watched as she held the brow of the young girl as the healer started to prepare his methods.

'She is moin malad anpil; it is dangerous for Sabrina. The Iwa could punish her.'

'Oungan will protect her' reported Sabrina's mother as she watched; forcing a smile away from her face.

They watched as he carried out the ritual, trusting that the healer would protect both girls so that this would not cause anything wrong to happen for the village. After a few days, the child got better, and many people thanked the healer for his help and asked about Sabrina. At this question, he smiled and looked at everyone directly.

'She is your next healer; she just had her first lesson.'

Over the next few years, Sabrina was taken under the wing of the oungan. Her apprenticeship was rigorous but essential; she passed through the ranks of the Vougan congregation until she was almost as equal as the oungan himself. She worked hard to make sure to afford the lessons she had; Sabrina harvested in the fields and worked with her mother at home.

'You must embrace konesans, you must be curious and look for new ways to develop your skill' her oungan would say to her at the end of every day she worked with him, he watched her curiosity with those who needed their help. She watched the way she eyes the ingredients for each ointment, thinking about what new product could be added to make a new or even better treatment. He would send her for writing appointments as she had a more fluent French hand than he did and he wanted her to make sure that was known before anything else, a good writer is hard to find in Haiti so when one is found, they are of great value and interest to the people.

When Sabrina went home, she would recount all that she learnt and would try to improve for the next day. She began advising many people with the help of her oungan; she would go to new patients before the healer arrived and examine them to try and work out what was wrong with them. By the time she was sixteen, she had started to become well known in her art form.

'I always knew my Sabrina would be my successful child, everyone doubted her, but I knew from the moment she was born' her mother would repeat to anyone who would listen to her.

This, as believed by Haitian, means that she is ready to become a healer. She started to excel in her apprenticeship, and the initiation ceremony had taken place. Many questioned her about what happened, but she couldn't risk losing her opportunity. It is strictly forbidden to reveal the events of initiation.

After the initiation, Sabrina was known as the local Manbo and demand for her, and the Oungan began to grow. She would travel to other villages that needed second opinions and was able to quickly earn money that paid off any debt she owed to the Oungan. Before her twentieth birthday, the Oungan fell ill. His sweat was so heavily that his forehead glimmered and reflected against the sun. Sabrina sat at his bedside and attempted to heal him with enchantments and anything she could think of.

'Sabrina, there's no point. My soul has passed on, and my body is ready to join it' smiled the Oungan holding her hand.

'I don't think I am ready to do this alone' Sabrina spoke clearly, ignoring the stinging pain in her eyes as she spoke.

They spoke at length the night before he died, they recalled all that they had seen together, recited scriptures and read to each other. The Oungan told her about the Iwa and how satisfied they were with her; his eyes started to darken as he stared at Sabrina's hand.

'You must be a careful child; these people will take advantage of you for your power. You must be strong and protect your family' he chanted.

Sabrina accepted this as a message from the Iwa. It was known that the Iwa would communicate with their people through the Oungan or Manbo, so Sabrina held this message within her and took care of it like a precious jewel. With the ending of this sentence, the Oungan closed his eyes and breathed lightly one last time. The candles in the room extinguished themselves violently with his last breath as if he had used it to blow out the candles.

After his death, Sabrina started to work harder to establish herself in the village. She became well known throughout the next few towns of Haiti as a talented healer. Sabrina became the first point of call for anyone's ailments; she began teaching young healers and working with others to improve their skills. She eventually earned enough money to purchase land and a better place to live so she could plant ingredients for her ointments. She was always busy and working to heal those in need.

CHAPTER 2

Sabrina eventually became so popular that she had to turn people away, and some would take advantage of her powers. They would ask for things she knew the Iwa would punish her for, like bringing someone back from the dead, or making someone who could not have a baby somehow fall pregnant. She had started to question the morals of those in her village and wondered what she could do to try to stop people taking advantage of her. Her family also frequently asked for predictions on the weather and if any disasters were about to come. Some people still disbelieved that she had the power of the Oungan and thought she merely copied his methods and the family paid him to teach her.

Sabrina had been working in the village for several years when she met Emmanuel Stevenson; he had travelled to her home with his younger sister, Chantel, seeking treatment. She had broken her arm in the recent flood, and they needed her healed so she could go to work in America and leave Haiti.

'I cannot show up on my first day with a broken wing; what will they think?' Chantel complained to Emmanuel who wanted her to wait a few more days to see Sabrina

Sabrina eyed the young man as she cared for his sister, binding her arms securely she asked too many questions about himself. She wondered why she had never seen him before, but with every question he rebuffed her. Sabrina eventually gave up trying to build a rapport with him and focused on healing Chantel. Once they were done, Emmanuel paid and carried his sister away

A few days later, Emmanuel came to the house, his legs were shaking, and his eyes darted around the room; unable to speak he muttered incoherently.

Sabrina had to focus on her breathing; she was becoming frustrated at his inability to speak.

'I want... I want to apologize, for-for my behavior.'

Sabrina raised her eyebrows, wrapping a blanket around her; she sat down fingering at the frayed thread in the blanket.

'I had been working late' 'You don't have to explain.'

'No, no I do, I had listened to the gossip around the village, but you healed my sister. I was also worried about that. '

'She's your sister, of course, you are worried.'

They spoke about the whispers around the village about her not being as powerful as she believed herself to be. Sabrina assured him of her abilities and spoke about healing her sister when she was a young child. A smile grew on her face, a common smile that usually occurs when you recall a fond memory, as she told the story and her fingers danced in the smoke of the fire in front of her. They bonded over childhood stories and spoke of their plans in life.

'You know they threaten me' Sabrina disclosed with a whisper 'The ones who spread the gossip that I am not a healer, they threaten me if I do not heal them or give them a service they need.'

They spoke into the evening and watched the sunset in the village. Neither of them wanted to stop talking, but they knew people would have seen Emmanuel enter the house.

'Can I come and see you again?' asked Emmanuel with a glimmer of hope, reflecting in his eyes as he looked at Sabrina.

Sabrina breathed in harshly and tilted her head to the side 'I'll have to see, there are so many appointments I have. But I promise I'll let you know.'

And with that evening started conversations worth two years and walks around the village, people began to talk and question Sabrina on her visits. They eventually became engaged and decided that Sabrina's home would be an excellent place to live together, in the village where they both worked, but far enough away that they were not under the constant eyes of the villagers.

Emmanuel, only then, became a target to the threats of the villagers. Every time Sabrina could not perform a ritual because it went against the wishes of the Iwa, or she gave a reading that the individual disagreed with, they would threaten her. They would threaten to kill her fiancé and to ruin her career. Every day she would then come home; tell Emmanuel about her day, she would lie with her head on his lap while he scratched her forehead and plaited her hair. The curls of her hair wrapped around his fingers like snakes. Sometimes the tears from her eyes would soak into his trousers and make his legs wet, which they would laugh about afterwards. She wanted to help everyone, but was eventually losing herself; she could feel herself drip out of her body. Her body and her soul were ripped apart, and she was trying to fix it, but she couldn't work out how to do it. Every threat pulled her more.

On one particular day, Sabrina had been threatened with the murder of her fiancé five times; she walked down the market feeling the eyes of the people of the village on her. She kept her head low and walked to her mother's house that was now surrounded by numerous grandchildren who threw themselves on Sabrina when they saw her approaching. She was unique to them; she would become magical and transform an everyday item into something much more enjoyable. Her mother smiled toothlessly as she saw Sabrina walking down the path, her sisters gossiped about their children and questioned Sabrina about her relationship.

'They won't accept that I can't help them, every time I refuse, they threaten me.'

The people of the village could not accept that a female denied them of anything, going ultimately against the beliefs of their religion. They wanted her to give them something exciting and change their life; they wanted to prepare for a next flood that might come or any other disaster. Her family listened in horror as she recounted the threats she received regularly and wanted to help in any way they can.

Her brothers asked for the names of those who threatened her, knowing that they would hurt anyone she had told. It was the same as when they were younger. As she was one of the youngest one among siblings, so she was protected by her siblings at the drop of a hat. She was also the one they judged the most, comparing their actions when they were her age to what she was now doing. Typical of Haiti, her family was close, and it was everything. They loved each other, but they also envied one another. Sabrina was the healer and one of their mother's favorites. Another had beautiful children, another had a brilliant reputation and was close nit with all the people of the village, and another was living in another country but was able to visit more frequently than those who lived in the next village. Their mother had eight children, and they all had something the other seven wanted or needed.

They told Sabrina to avoid those who were threatening her and thinking back to what the Oungan once told her and did when he was threatened. It helped her to think about her old teacher; she had been thinking about leaving and giving up on her career. She walked home, holding her head up, not noticing the people staring at her in disapproval and someone lurking in the shadows watching her. She bought her usual supplies for dinner she was going to make Emmanuel ready for Chantel's arrival. She came loaded with suitcases and bags packed so full you could hear the breaking of the zippers on the side of the suitcase.

'You're here for a week, not moving in' laughed Emmanuel as he grabbed one of the suitcases that arched his arm as he went to pick it up. He groaned and felt his arm click as he strained the suitcase into the truck.

The smell of Sabrina's food climbed throughout the village and intoxicated the senses of Emmanuel and Chantel as they walked up to Sabrina's home. They sat and caught up with each other, gossiping about America and the life of Haiti. Chantel was unsurprised that the village had not changed since she had left two years previously, the marks of the flooding had sunk into the bottom of the huts. She noticed the darkness that had ensnared the village since she had gone, the flooding had drowned the purity of the village and allowed cruelty and desperation to fester and feed on any remaining virtue the village had left.

Sabrina went about her work, enjoying the time she had with her fiancé and her family and aiming to brush off threats and forgive those who sought to harm her. She looked forward to the healing of a young child she had been helping for several weeks and to place a healing ceremony for an individual who needed some help at home. She continued to ignore those who had threatened her and looked forward to detailing her day to those who were waiting for her at home.

'Murder'

'Murder' was echoing throughout the village, cries and screams had replaced the usual hubbub of the people. Sabrina jumped in her place when she heard this, they looked to the horizon, expecting yet another wave of water to engulf the recently build houses of the last flood. She checked herself and listened to the screams. They were calling murder, Sabrina felt a twisting inside her, she felt sick, and her head pounded, she knew the Iwa wasn't happy. A death that was unexpected by them was always met with anger and torment. They wanted justice, and they knew it would be dealt with.

Sabrina could hear a faint screaming which alerted her more when she realized it was Chantel. She walked in the direction of the screaming, memorizing what to do. She had only learned in theory about the protocols regarding murder; she was so deep in her own thoughts that she did not notice the hard steps approaching her until a rough hand gripped tightly onto Sabrina's arm and pushed her hard against the wall.

'We warned you' growled a masked individual who snarled at her with hatred.

'We warned you what would happen if you denied us what we needed' he snarled again before pushing away from her and running away, with a bloodied knife in hand.

Shaking fearfully and breathing erratically, Sabrina sunk to the floor of the alleyway. Some mud from the hut she lent on marked her clothes; tears sprang to her eyes that she desperately tried to hold back. She always looked awful after she cried, and she knew the stains on her cheeks would fail her.

She strained to stand up and walked in the direction of the screams, longing for her bed and to see Emmanuel. She saw people crowding her home where the screams were coming from and rolled her eyes.

'People can't leave my family alone, can they?' she thought to herself as she walked towards her home before she realized what her attacker had just said to her.

A cold feeling rushed throughout her body, and her stomach lurched again, she started to walk through the crowd who tried to hold her back and prevent her from entering the house. Upon eventually arriving in her home, she saw Chantel sitting on the floor her eyes red and raw as if she had rubbed them away. Her mouth looked broken from screaming, her mother was holding her firm, and the police were in the bathroom mumbling to themselves and another consoling Chantel and her family. Sabrina's eyes widened as she dreaded what she would say when she entered the bathroom. A police officer barred her entrance; she explained that this was her home, and she demanded to be let in.

She entered the bathroom to see a pool of water full of blood, and her fiancé sat in the bath, with stab wounds to his chest.

CHAPTER 3

A few hours beforehand, Sabrina was with yet another family. She had conducted a healing ceremony on a family with a young child that had been taken ill. The family had three girls who stood and watched their younger sister being healed in awe, Sabrina was used to this as every child believed they were magical healers. They tried to copy Sabrina's actions thinking they could help heal their sister, twirling and singing, placing cloths of water on her head. The home filled with laughter and ritualistic singing. The baby occasionally cried and coughed at the incense that burned in the corner of the room.

'It is the illness leaving her body, her body is helping us' Sabrina chanted when the baby's mother attempted to quite the screaming.

As Sabrina moved around her chanting and applying an appropriate treatment of the child. Their mother breathed heavily when her baby was healed; she held her belly, which was only just showing that a new child was on the way.

As Sabrina was leaving, father of the girls chased after her. 'I need to ask you something.'

Sabrina smiled warmly 'I need you to make sure my next child is a boy; I need a boy.'

Sabrina questioned whether, to tell the truth, although the threats were still in the back of her mind, she knew the Iwa would be unhappy if she meddled with their wishes. She was afraid of his reaction as she knew he would be disappointed.

'I can't; the Iwa would not be happy.'

He stood and stared at Sabrina for a minute 'I need a boy if you don't give me one, you will lose something you love dearly.'

He walked away, angrily into the distance, cursing her angrily under his breath, while he entered the house. As Sabrina walked away, she heard the slam of the home's door and the quiet shouting of an angry man who had been once again denied. She looked around fearfully, dreading anyone hearing his anger, but she was so panicked that she still couldn't notice a figure lurking in the shadows. They followed her home, inspecting her every move as they did every night. They knew her routine by now, but it started at first as mere intimidation, but desperation had eaten away at the families asking what Sabrina could not deliver. Later Sabrina would question how them turning to murderer would please the Iwa enough to give what they wanted. It was getting too much for people, their needs and wants had become mixed, and greed was the result.

Sabrina walked home to Emmanuel, who had been preparing his work during his break. His hands were rough with eczema which had flared up when the threats bean. When she arrived home, Emmanuel immediately could tell that something was not right, her face was crumpled like an old piece of paper and it burned like an old cinder. She would later recall angrily retelling Emmanuel what had just happened. Recounting what the man had said to her 'I am falling out of love with this; I used to adore my work, be so grateful for this gift. But now I don't know what to do' she cried bitterly into his shoulder as he kissed her forehead and soothed her cries. He wanted desperately to take away the pain of what these people would say to her on a daily basis, but he knew he couldn't.

They sat in silence for a moment, neither of them knowing what to say or do, holding each other's hands and looking into the horizon as they did every day.

'Why don't you go back out, treat your final few people and come home? My friends are coming over soon, but they should be gone by the time you come back, and Chantel is doing some work in her room so we can just have a nice evening together. How does that sound?'

Sabrina got up and smiled at Emmanuel, tears on her cheeks shining gleefully before she wiped them away. She agreed to go back out, before leaving they hugged each other and comforted each other for a while before she left. As she walked back down into the village, Sabrina thought back to the frist time she came home to him, with a massive grin on his face and a dinner beautifully cooked. Before the house finally went out of view, she turned around again to get one final glance, feeling the warmth of happiness rise in her body. It was the final time she would have this emotion, and it was as if her body knew and wanted to savor this emotion while she still could.

The next time she saw the front door was the horrible night of Emmanuel's death.

She walked into the bathroom wide-eyed and saw Emmanuel, lying open- eyed in the bath, blood still seeping from the wounds of the stab marks to his chest. The water intermingling with the blood and turning it a light red. His body was lying floating in the water like a piece of driftwood. The smell of blood made the air rancid and turned Sabrina's stomach. She tried to cry and show emotion, but Chantel seemed to be taking most of the tears up. Sabrina went and sat with her in-law family, puzzling over why their Emmanuel was gone. No one spoke to Sabrina, and they knew she wouldn't listen. She replayed the message from the masked man before she arrived at home and decided to secure the house.

'Too late now' she thought to herself, she had no one else to protect now.

Chantel was going to her family's home, so the house was just to herself.

Sabrina then sent away the spectators who were still gossiping outside the house, when Emmanuel's friends arrived at the door. They had reached the central part of the village when they also heard the murder cries and came to see what the matter was.

'Sabrina, what's happened?' they called looking around the house. Sabrina looked at the three men, all of a similar build to Emmanuel - meeting each other at work typically had that effect. She couldn't see them without expecting Emmanuel in tow with them. Usually, they would be laughing together about something at work. Their silence and stern faces made her uncomfortable.

They walked into the house and helped family to clean up in silence. Sabrina kissed Emmanuel's forehead as he was being taken to the morgue for examination. The rest of them could barely look at him; his face had distorted from the water in which he was submerged. Chantel had been taken to the family home to sleep, and it was finally just Sabrina and the boys in her home. They wanted to protect her, who knew if the killer would come back and she was sure to be the next victim. She told them about the threats she had received.

'How was he when you saw him?' Sabrina asked; she thought back to the last exchange with him. The love she felt for him, and the excitement of seeing Emmanuel had filled up inside her as she had approached the home, only to be destroyed.

They spoke about how they drank and ate some food while talking about their lives as they usually had. Emmanuel had told them about the threats Sabrina had been receiving.

'And now I am being followed' he had said to them, looking each of them deeply in the eye as he spoke.

He had been followed on the way to collect Chantel three days beforehand, and every time he turned his back when he wandered through the village, it was as if Emmanuel was constantly being watched.

The men then continued to recount what they believed they had seen after leaving Sabrina's house. On their walk home, they had seen an unusual individual walking up the path to the house, he had been dressed in dark clothing, half covering his face which was not unheard of in the village. They called greetings towards him, but none were returned. He seemed to be carrying something in his hand, though at the time they couldn't work out what.

'It was like a shadow' one of the men said to Sabrina after a few moments of silence, they buried their heads in their hands struggling to even look Sabrina in the face as she waited for further explanation.

They continued to describe how they had heard shuffling noises opposite the house, at the time it was passed off as an animal. But now they weren't so sure 'So, you think that the murderer was waiting for you to leave?' Sabrina questioned them Silence fell upon the home again, no one said anything for what felt like hours. The men offered to stay with Sabrina for the night, even offered for her to come and live in their respective houses for a while, but

Sabrina knew her place was here. The Iwa needed to be given offerings for forgiveness and she had to conduct a ritual before the day was over, and she wanted to do it alone.

CHAPTER 4

That night was the hardest in Sabrina's life, the heavy weight of Emmanuel against her back as she slept was missing, and her bed felt empty and cold without him. For a moment, she was sure she heard his breath or felt his arms around her, but she knew it was the only delusion. She watched rays of the sun enter her bedroom and shine against her face. The morning was usually the best part of her day, with Emmanuel, they would watch the sunrise and talk about all of their plans together. She thought back to the day before, how in the morning she had kissed him lightly and ungratefully; before leaving to go about her daily business, like an old chore, absent-minded. A kiss was all she longed for now, to smell him in a big embrace and to know that she was safe in the world as long as he was there. Now he was gone, the world was cold and dangerous. Shadows were now everywhere, and darkness had even touched her, her eyes had turned black overnight from the glorious brown they once were. They were a vortex of nothing but hatred and despair.

Sabrina rose from her bed, her head feeling heavy but her feet were lightly touching the floor. She plodded into her kitchen where gifts and offerings of food to the Iwa had been left to ask for forgiveness. Food had also been given to her, some of those who had threatened her before, now were coming to her home to offer advice and their condolences. Sabrina knew they were merely doing one of two things, reveling in her misery or trying to make sure Sabrina knew that they had nothing to do with Emmanuel's murder. She hated them and she stared at their food with the same feelings. She walked into the village and went about her daily healing business, no one dared to ask about Emmanuel, and she did not mention him. That is to say; he was not mentioned as soon as Sabrina left the homes of the unwell people.

As Sabrina walked throughout the winding paths of the village, she eventually bumped into Chantel at about 10 am. Wrinkles had appeared on her face that hadn't been there the day before, and the skin under her eyes was flaking like a bad case of eczema from crying.

'Chantel where are you going?'

'I've got to go to the police station and make a statement' said Chantel with her head down and walking away in the direction of the police precinct.

'You should too, and sooner the better' she hissed into Sabrina's ear. Sabrina watched Chantel as she walked away and wondered whether she should journey now with her, thinking it would be better to tell the police about the threats sooner rather than later.

The police station was more akin to an old shack when Chantel arrived, it was painted yellow and had more protection against floods than any other building in the Haiti village. She picked at her raw bitten nails as she waited for an interview with the police officers. Thinking over what happened the night before and lamenting over the last words she said to her brother - they were nothing, but now they will remain in her memory until the day she too would die. She thought back to when they were children and remembered how death was a common thing in her family, and her brother was not afraid of it as he would almost cheat death, but now his luck was gone and his final gamble was over.

Once Chantel was in the interview room, she could not focus anymore on what has happened; her family had questioned her all night. The image of her brother dead in a bath all she could see it was like a horror film she knew the ending, and she knew the beginning, but she couldn't pause it; she couldn't escape from the guilt of what happened the night before. The police went about their usual method of questioning, which helped Chantel be able to record officially what had occurred in her point of view. She told them about her life in America and her relationship with her brother; as she found the body, she knew she was the Prime Suspect.

'So, if you now live in America, why are you here, in your future sister-in- law's house?'

'I came to see my brother and Sabrina; I like to think I'm the main reason the two of them are together, and before I left for America, we used to hang out all the time. I missed home, and I wanted to come back for a while. Work allowed me to relocate back to Haiti, I supposed to tell my brother today but obviously, I can't now -'

Chantel then closed off very rapidly; she imagined all the things she said about Emmanuel was another wound to him. She wanted to get away, but she couldn't work out on how. The investigators continue asking questions; they offered her refreshment and talked about daily life to try and calm her down and make her more co-operative. Her lawyer had arrived and was encouraging her to speak, knowing that not helping police would make her look more guilty. She then began to recount the events of the night before. She Told them about Sabrina coming home in tears and telling Emmanuel about the threats she had received again.

'Threats?' The officer asked, leaning further towards Chantel as he reached into his pocket to start taking notes again.

Chantel continued including everything she knew about the threats Sabrina had been receiving. She began chewing on the top of her lip, trying to decipher what would happen to her brother. She then went on to say that three friends came to visit Emmanuel. They sat and drank for a few hours while she was in her bedroom. The officer asked if anything suspicious was heard while they were there.

Chantel shook her head solemnly and did not reply; however, after a while, she frowned and looked up towards the ceiling. She remembered her brother telling his friends he was afraid because he was being followed. By this point, the police officer was scribbling violently on his notepad, as a plethora of questions had arisen, and he wanted to make sure that he had not missed a single one. Chantel then continued stating that her brother and his friends then brushed off this confession and continued laughing into the night. The threats were not mentioned again, and the figure in the shadows following him was ignored. Chantel remembered having thought to herself to say something to her brother after they had gone.

'Now' the police officer interrupted, 'was he still alive when the friends left?'

Chantelle nodded more enthusiastically now; she heard them all calling goodbye to each other as they always did before they turned towards their respective homes. She watched them leave into the darkness noticing how the light reflected, on some of their faces and not on others as the moonlight cast a hazy shadow on the house which reflected into the street below.

After they left, Chantel went to find her brother to ask him about what he had told his friends. As she left her bedroom, she noticed a slight noise in the shadows opposite the house, but when she went to her window, there was nothing to be seen. She walked into the living room of Sabrina's home to question her brother. He was washing up from food and drinks consumed while his friends were there and seemed to be entirely in his own thoughts. She could hear her brother humming silently to himself; it wasn't a pleasant hum, but more of an absent-minded sound that rung in her ears as she continued to speak to the police officer.

He barely noticed her walk into the room and jumped violently when she said his name, the hum had vanished like a clear mist. Emmanuel laughed and coughed slightly when he says, Chantel.

'It was like he was expecting someone else to be there' she recounted staring through the police officer and onto the wall behind him; shaking her head as if refusing any tears that tried to make an appearance. They spoke for a few minutes about what he had been seeing, Chantel could tell that he was not indeed himself, he was usually so bubbly and warm, but tonight he was frank and cold, his body rigid and he seemed so much smaller to her than ever before. Not long afterwards, Emanuel announced that he was tired and would have a nap before Sabrina came home. He wanted to be there for her and decided that being tired would not help either of their mental states.

Chantel watched her brother shuffle his feet along the floor as she entered the dark bedroom on the other side of the corridor and listened for the squeaking of the door as it shut behind him. She then went about cleaning anything that Emanuel had left - he never indeed was a good cleaner - and decided to secure the windows of the house shut to give the family privacy. If it were true what Emanuel said, then it would have been possible that her actions were being watched. Back in the interview room, she was not sure if that was the right decision. Every time she told a new detail, she paused slightly questioning if that tiny detail could have prevented the little outcome.

'I would like to go home now' announced Chantel, as she pressed her hands against the table for leverage to rise. She could not stand without support ever since she saw her brother's body. It was as if her strength had died with him and left a carcass of what used to be, just like with Emmanuel now.

After a while, Chantel decided she too would go to bed, when there was a knock on the door. Behind the door was a man she almost recognized in a dark coat and gloves. When thinking back to it, Sabrina would curse herself thinking that she should have known what was coming next, but she was tired and didn't want to cause a fuss.

The individual explained that he was a neighbour and wondered if he could use the bathroom; this was a common thing in this village. The rainfall frequently ruined the drains so toilets sometimes would stop working, and as a native to Haiti, Chantel would have known this. She allowed the individual into the home, and she attempted to guide him to a bathroom, but it seemed as if he already knew where the bathroom was. He entered the bathroom, and Chantel was confident that she heard the bathroom violently locking.

After a while she heard water splashing, assuming the individual was merely washing his hands, she ignored it and carried on with work, it was not until after ten minutes of complete silence that she believed anything was wrong.

She walked over the bathroom door and knocked to see if anyone would answer.

No answer.

She looked at the clock, Sabrina would be home in 20 minutes, and she didn't want her to come home to a neighbour in her house when the pair were already on edge about being stalked. She knocked again

No answer

Chantel groaned quietly to herself; she went to open the door. She felt the lock stop her hand halfway through the twist. She could feel a slight breeze coming through the window of the bathroom. She struggled to open the door again when she heard something that sounded like running go past the house and into the darkness.

CHAPTER 5

Chantel then carried on describing what happened next to the police officer; she was surprised to remember everything in as much detail as if she were living it again. She recalled how she frowned and thought to herself about what to do; she looked around where she was trying to find something that maybe could help gain access into the bathroom. Chantel heard the faint drop of water falling into the bath from the tap above and listened for any more movement. She walked quickly into the kitchen, searching for something to wedge the door open, even slightly. She ran her hands through all the drawers in the kitchen and even looked in the spice pots where Sabrina kept her ointment ingredients. Nothing could be found. The floor was cold on the bottom of her feet, and the silence in the empty house made her sensitive to any other noise that may intrude into the home.

She had attempted to pick the lock on the bathroom door; it was one of the old-fashioned types with gaping keyholes. They seemed easy enough to decipher on the outside, but they never were as easy. They were unpredictable to someone who had no idea what to do. She tried to use a screwdriver to push the lock back, but nothing seemed to work. Chantel huffed heavily and slumped onto the floor, she grabbed her face and left her fingernails scratch her forehead, leaving red marks. Defeated, she pressed her ear to the wooden door, trying desperately to decipher any noise she possibly could. They pushed her body onto the floor and peered through the small gap between the door and the floor, a little beacon of light came through, and some splashes of water had fallen on the floor. The wind from the window, that for some reason was open, was blowing in Chantel's face.

'Why did you think there was water on the floor?' the police officer interrupted, listening intently as he watched Chantel fiddle with a hangnail on her finger.

'I dunno' she said, looking down at her finger and pursing her lips.

She then carried on, recalling how she groaned as she rose from the floor and attempted to find out when anyone was there. Before her fist connected the door with a vicious thud, she heard a strange noise, which she thought was in the bathroom but now she wasn't so sure. Chantel thought about the murderers while retelling the story, laughing at her as she naively attempted to save her brother's life.

'I listened out for another sound, thinking maybe the neighbour - well who I thought was a neighbour - had been in an accident. I waited for maybe two more minutes and then knocked on the door again.'

There was no noise coming from the door but a slight drop of water into the bath and a splash of water from the tub onto the floor, that occasionally would fall so violently that it would rebound out of the bathroom and onto the floor in the hallway.

'Emmanuel!' called Chantel after there still was no answer; she had heard a loud rusting outside when she knocked. As if she had disturbed someone spying.

She waited for an answer, but nothing came to her, still sat on the floor with her hand on the door she peered into the dark bedroom where she believed Emmanuel was. She covers seemed to have been thrown over, but she couldn't see anything else. She shuffled in the direction of the bedroom and called to him again. A cold chill ran throughout her body as she tried to work out what was happening.

'It was then that I realized that they were right; they were right to be scared and paranoid. The house is eerie when it's quiet, and all you can hear is the light thumping of your heart' she reported to the policeman.

She pulled herself slowly up to go to her brother's bedroom; she cursed herself, knowing he would tell her off for waking him up and bringing a stranger into the house. She saw the moonlight again shining into the bedroom, turning it into the abstract blue that most people mistake for black. She knocked on the bedroom door lightly and called him again. When she entered the bedroom, she saw that the bed was empty and cold, the sheet on the mattress had wrinkled and caved in where Emmanuel and Sabrina slept. There were books of medicine, Voodoo idols and symbols throughout the bedroom, with candles at different stages of melting and burning surrounding the bedroom. There were clothes strewn about the bedroom and papers stacked in the corner of the room.

Chantel could feel her breath starting to become erratic; she expected her brother to be in his bed. She continued to call his name and searched around the house. Maybe he had gone out, she thought to herself. Or perhaps she had merely missed him walking around the house like she missed the man leaving the house. She continued to look around the bedroom, searching for clues, maybe his keys or his wallet was gone. She was so preoccupied in her own thoughts that she ignored the unlocking of the bathroom door and a dark individual exiting the bathroom, with a knife in hand and locking the door behind him. Leaving a wet footprint on the floor as he left that the police would later notice. He closed the door slightly and carefully just as he had done with the bathroom window and locked it from the outside. He had duplicated the key from his last break-in at the house.

The intruder heard a shuffle from the bedroom door and escaped before Chantel noticed what was happening. She walked out of the bedroom two seconds later, focused on her search for Emmanuel, not seeing the key that had been left in the bathroom or the intruder jumping quietly closing the front door of the home.

Chantel walked around the home, delicately putting both hands into the mess of her hair as she pulled it up into a bun and secured it with a pin.

'Emmanuel?' Chantel called again, her voice breaking halfway through; as her eyes frantically roamed around the living room

Chantel turned towards the bathroom door again and walked towards it to try to investigate, her feet padding on the floor as she went. She raised her fist to knock on the door when she finally noticed the golden key standing from the keyhole. She inhaled sharply and shook her head. She tried to remember back to before, but she was sure that there was no key. She hyperventilated sharply, and her jaw dropped so violently that it still ached to talk the next day. 'What did you think when you saw the key?' the police officer asked,

Chantel had gone quiet again and he could see her lip quivering as she struggled to get the words out.

'I'm not sure; I was confused. I could still see the tools I had used to pick the lock, but they had water droplets on them' Chantel recalled blankly as if she was reading aloud a shopping list.

Chantel had then tried to open the door, which turned loosely in her hand but then slammed shut again. She pulled her hand away and ran into the village, there was no longer a shadow, but there were wet footprints now on the path in which Chantel followed. She ran home and into the home of her next brother, whom she had seen the day before.

'You have to help me' Chantel announced slamming back with the front door.

She explained what had happened that evening, the threats, the intruder and so on. Within minutes her brother and his friends were running with her to Sabrina's home, the door had been left open, and the golden rectangle from the light inside was shining like a lighthouse guiding them to the scene. They walked into the home, all the boys wielding weapons ready to discover what had happened.

'Darius' Chantel whispered through her teeth 'be careful, please' her eyes had widened to compete with the moon that was still shining brilliantly into the night—naively trying to comfort those in Sabrina's home who were about to discover a gruesome sight. The boys walked closer to the bathroom, twisted the cold key and threw the door open.

Darius gazed into the dark bathroom and turned the light on; no one was there. He walked

slightly into the bathroom, then looked at Chantel.

'You idiot' he said, walking briskly towards his sister 'you wasted my time, learn how to be more aware - 'he was interrupted by one of his friends calling to him. They had gone in to investigate the room when he saw what had happened on the other side of that door.

Darius pushed off of Chantel and walked towards his friend, who was pointing in the direction of the bathtub that still had a dripping tap. There were leaves from a tree outside the bathroom and mud on the windowsill. They had found Emmanuel. He was lying in the bath that had now run cold; his skin had gone wrinkly typical of someone who had been in the tub for a long time. His skin was pale but still warm, and his eyes were closed. The water he was sitting in had turned pink with the blood, and the white tub had been stained with his blood which took hours to clean up after the body had been taken.

'Darius? What's wrong?' Chantel called, creeping slowly towards the bathroom where Darius stood staring at whatever was in the bathroom. She reached the bathroom door when her brother shoved her away with one hand. She could hear another of Darius' friends running through the village shouting murder as he ran in the direction of the police station. The murderer was still sitting in the darkness opposite the home, reveling in the panic he had caused, and a cruel, disturbing smile appeared on his face. He looked down at the bloodied knife and cursed himself; there was only one knife in his hand. Where was the other one? He started to run in the direction of his home; now the alarm had been sounded it was a matter of time before people would arrive.

On his run down the hill, he was Sabrina walking suspiciously up the mountain; she had heard the calls by now.

Darius was pushing Chantel back repeatedly, trying to stop her from seeing her beloved brother in such an awful state.

'Let me see' she screamed, scratching at Darius' face and pushing him equally as hard as he was pushing her.

After a while, he, tired of her cries and grabbed her face and shook it.

'If I let you look, you must keep calm. People are coming to help. Okay?' Darius snarled before letting go of her face to wipe a tear from his own cheek. His teeth were hurting from gritting them so violently, and he couldn't bear to fight anymore. Chantel was led into the bathroom, the last time she saw her brother he was smiling slightly and walking tiredly to his bedroom. Now he was lying with his mouth open and looking up at the ceiling.

Chantel finished the interview as solemnly as she started it. The room was now stagnant with murdered air; while the police officer finished his report and the lawyer finished writing Chantel's final statement. She rose from the table and saw herself in the mirror, or what she believed to be herself. She had aged from the night before, and her body was as empty of blood as her brother's. Chantel climbed down the stairs into the village, where a crowd had gathered to wish her well, her brothers had pushed the spectators away to let their sister get through. They placed their arms around Chantel and led her home.

CHAPTER 6

Sabrina was now all alone in a quiet, now haunted, home. She eyes the idols and symbols to the Iwa and questioned why she was punished, she was loyal to the rules of the Iwa, and she lost her fiancé in the process. The corridor stank heavily of bleach from Sabrina's continual washing of the bath, nothing made it feel clean, and the red stains from Emmanuel's blood were still prominent. Sabrina arose with the sun again and carried Emmanuel's jumper in his hands, it still smelled like him, and for a second, she would forget he was gone. She wanted to work out how to make a potion to make the scent of him permanent, but she did not know how. She walked around the home, trying to remember what she did in the mornings; the thought of eating would hurt her soul. Everything tasted of salt to her, even the sweetest cakes.

She started looking around her home as if it was the first time she had ever been there. If she inspected the house, she thought, she could find her purpose again or some reason. All she found was dust and bleach intermingling. Until she went outside the front door, underneath the window in which the suspect had jumped through two nights ago was the other knife. The police knew that there were two weapons used, the different wounds indicated as such. It was dried and covered in blood, she couldn't bring herself to touch it, and she couldn't believe that the suspects had not come back for it. Either they knew they would get away with the murder, or they were too stupid to come looking for it.

'Could that be the second weapon?' Sabrina asked the police officer

The police had come to the house and removed the weapon taking it back into the station to be investigated. They had found more information about the case, but Sabrina could tell they knew the investigation was going to be difficult. After the police left, Sabrina went about going to her work. The villagers could barely look her in the eye, and those who did could see that she had died on the inside with Emmanuel. She avoided questions that rarely came and eyed the useless ring on her finger from Emmanuel. She couldn't remember what he looked like anymore, it had only been a few days, but all she could see was the wasted life in the bathroom. She needed to get away.

Eventually, Emmanuel's body was released to the family and had been allowed to be buried. The autopsy report had been made and filed, and there was nothing more to be done with him. Sabrina viewed his body when it returned home in a pale wooden coffin; his forehead was soaked with her tears as she kissed his forehead lightly. He looked peaceful even though his last moments would have been full of pain; you couldn't tell on the body. The body indicated what was already known. He had been stabbed at least ten times while he was in the bath. Chantel and Sabrina were both confused as to why it had not been noticed that he was in the bathroom, but for one thing, it was confirmed that whoever went into the bathroom had killed Emmanuel. Chantel would never forgive herself for this fact.

A duplicate of the knife was purchased and measured, it accounted for 6 of the stab wounds, and another four were given by the blade still in possession of the murderer. It was concluded that there had to have been two assailants that night. One knife had a brutal amount of force behind it, accurately attacking the heart, but the other had no pressure; it was sloppy work and made the murder much longer than it should be.

'It didn't go to plan' one of the detectives decided upon examining the autopsy.

There was a gap between wounds, as would be expected, but it seems like the individual who had pretended to be a neighbour dealt the more damaging and powerful blows after another person had failed to kill Emmanuel. But he was dead for around an hour before his body was found.

'The main problem is that this is no abstract knife used; this is a common kitchen knife—thousands like them. If we searched the homes of the villagers, they most likely all would have the knife we are looking for' another police officer announced somberly.

'There had also been fragments of the bigger knife that had broken off upon impact, the knife we are looking for would not be completely intact.'

The police, in this case, argued over theories for days, less investigation was being done, and the family was getting limited information about the issue. Sabrina's spirit had gone entirely; she was so thin that her body ached with every slight motion, and the thought of sleep would hurt. Half her home was inaccessible as the memories were too raw, Emmanuel's mother's scream echoed throughout the house and rang away at night, stopping Sabrina from sleeping.

'Why not come home?' Sabrina's mother suggested after visiting the house, which looked abandoned and unloved. She had never seen her daughter so thin, even after floods that devastated the harvest, she never looked so depleted of life.

Sabrina scoffed at the idea; she couldn't stand the sympathetic faces her sisters would give her - she knew they would in some way be happy something had finally gone wrong for her. They liked Emmanuel, but their pride and jealousy were more important to them than common decency most of the time. Sabrina continued to live as quietly and isolated as she could, she had started to lose people's custom, believing the Iwa cursed her. She could not see a way out of this, and she wanted to be out. She wanted to stop the pain in her chest; she wanted her mind to be quiet for a few moments. Ritual upon ritual was performed, and she read obsessively for answers, in vain.

A fortnight after Emmanuel's death, Sabrina and her fiancé's family had become impatient. It was as if the entire case had been forgotten about or the police were letting the murderer get away with it. They called the leader of the police force and made sure that the case was going to be treated with respect.

'My son would never hurt anyone, but he had been killed, and you are treating it like nothing' his mother yelled down the phone, she always knew what she wanted, and she got it too. Everyone in the community loved her or at least pretended to - either out of fear or respect no one really knew. She had piled her hair high above her head and stormed to the office after her call. Her shouting could be heard from miles away, and it gave comfort to Sabrina as she went about her day.

It was not only the police who had forgotten about the murder but the people had too. Chantel had returned to America early to avoid meeting the same fate, and no one other than Emmanuel's mother would mention his death. Sabrina had got more healings and was being asked to perform inappropriate rituals again. With each request, Sabrina became more conflicted; she believed that she was being punished for something with Emmanuel's death, and she feared the consequences again. She had refused to answer most of the requests and the memories of the man attacking her, and the threats were still raw and heavy.

They were still raw when she repeated them to the police, who had been harassed and abused so heavily by Emmanuel's mother that they had to investigate the case. Police officers strolled about the village, asking everyone Sabrina reported about their threats and their means to carry out the murder. Kitchen utensils were seized, and homes were searched, people were interviewed and arrested. But to no avail. Their main question now was why? Emmanuel was a well-loved man, so why such a brutal attack against him?

The customers who threatened Sabrina weeks ago were now visiting her home to apologize, which was always ended with a slam of the front door and Sabrina rolling her eyes when they left. After a while, everyone who had threatened her was now apologizing to her. While they spoke, she looked deeply into their eyes and tried to recognize their voice from the attacker with the bloodied knife. With every visit, she hated the village more. Their visits had muddied her memory of that night, each one could have been the man, and each one wasn't. Every night Sabrina would crawl into her bed defeated, her scalp aching from her pulling at her hair so much and she had a cold sore from always biting her chapped and bleeding lips. She couldn't live in constant torment any longer. And she started to conspire. She couldn't live in the house anymore, and she certainly could not stay in the village like a lamb waiting for slaughter.

By the time Sabrina had sold her home and moved somewhere no one else knew about, the police had released a final piece of information that they thought would comfort the family. They had done some other exams, to see if someone had irritated Emmanuel when they walked into the bathroom and provoked the murderer. It was discovered that Emmanuel had fallen asleep in the bath before he was murdered. Therefore, felt nothing. The first stabbing had, in fact, killed him but it appeared not to. From this fact, the police knew that this was either a panicked killing or a first killing; from this knowledge, a weight had been lifted from Sabrina's heart. It was as if for a moment she felt happiness, her thoughts had tormented over the pain Emmanuel would have felt during his last moments, and now they could be quieted. He was not scared.

The family wandered around the village for a while, eyeing over everyone who lived there. The trust and love that was once felt in this village had been ripped apart by greed and needs just like the floods had ripped away at their homes. The smiles on the villagers were no longer precious, and their happiness meant nothing to Emmanuel's family. One by one, the family moved away, Darius moved to another village where he was able to work, and the siblings followed. The last one to leave the village was Emmanuel's headstrong mother, but now she had wilted like a suffocated flower, and she haunted the village with her anger and misery. Before leaving, she had one last conversation with Sabrina.

'I see him all the time, Sabrina' she said, leaning on Sabrina's arm.

'Me too, the Iwa has gifted me with being able to speak to him' she confided in her, she looked at the ground outside of her new home and kicked the dust of the earth at the front of her door.

'You must have pleased them in some way then, child' his mother smiled, cupping Sabrina's face like Emmanuel once did. She knew it would be a struggle for Sabrina to be on her own now, she had tormented herself for days about whether it was the best thing to do.

Chantel had suffered a nervous breakdown after returning to her job in America and needed support. The only one who could go was her mother; it would be good for her to see a new place, she thought as she packed her bags for America. Haiti had become a stranger to her; the floods had ripped away any landmarks she used to recognize where she was, and the murder of her son had darkened her heart to those who had tormented her son in life and now were tormenting herself and Sabrina in his death.

Sabrina watched the last trace of Emmanuel, and left Haiti the next morning; she was alone now. No one could protect her now. Her own family had practically abandoned her and told her to get over Emmanuel's death and move on. The sympathy had dried up and, it seemed, so had their love for her.

CHAPTER 7

As the weeks went on, the idea that Emmanuel's case would be solved began to dwindle. His murder had become old news and his family was gone. The only constant reminder of Emmanuel was Sabrina. She haunted the village with her slightly low hanging head and her sunken eyes. Sabrina had a boring life she had no purpose anymore she would go and conduct healings or her rituals and go home, where she would try to eat and fail and then she would have broken sleep. Nightmares were the only company she had, and she began welcoming them like an old friend.

The police had ceased their investigation, as the threats from Emmanuel's mother were now gone, it made sense not to try with a case. They never really liked healers, they interfered with the investigation and one of the senior police officers never really believed Sabrina had the powers she said she had.

'Then why doesn't she just magic him back then if she's so upset' he would laugh throwing the case away from him as he slumped into a chair.

The case had lost all its meaning to the officers due to his attitude so they dispensed with interviews and labeled it 'Cold Case' in a marker - the same dark red as the bloodstains on the bathtub in Sabrina's house.

Sabrina walked through the village; one day on her walk home after a busy day and stumbled upon the market. Vegetables and spices and sweet pastries decorated the air with a concocted scent that stained the nostrils for days afterwards. As she walked through the market, she was aware of people talking, looking at her but then turning away when she looked at them. They would laugh to themselves quietly as she walked past. The people of the village had seemed to forget her power and that they were once her friends. Jealousy seemed to have consumed them and their humanity had depleted.

Sabrina went to a stall to purchase some spices and herbs for the ointments, they avoided eye contact with her and avoided unnecessary conversation.

'Sabrina' one of her sisters called after she saw her in the market and the villagers watching her with contempt.

'Come to our house, you look so unwell, please. We'll look after you' she smiled, holding her hand. The two of them were the closest of the siblings, they had a strong bond being only a year apart in age. Sabrina had started to gain colour in her skin again and had started to eat slightly, even if it was thin chicken broth.

She refused the offer, she felt safe in her isolated home. She could live her own way without being under the constant scrutiny of the villagers. Her sister lived next to the town gossip, who would hang through the window of the main room and gather all the information she could. If the windows were covered, she would bang hard on the window calling her name.

They both decided it would be better for her to stay at her home.

'At least come and eat dinner with us so I know you are eating' she fussed, raising her eyebrows as she moved her head to the side

Sabrina smiled and agreed to this at least.

'You should have listened to our threats' shouted a villager randomly, smiling smugly to themself. This was one of the people who had come to apologize to Sabrina weeks earlier. This confirmed to her, that none of the apologies were sincere but merely self-serving.

The healings had started to come back to their normal genre, again showing that Emmanuel's death meant nothing. They asked too much of her and when she couldn't deliver in time, they would become verbally aggressive and threaten her family again. She would go home, frustrated scratching her forehead and baring her teeth, she hated her job and needed to punish the ones who were hurting her.

'Well if the police aren't going to do anything, I will have to'

The next day, Sabrina had an appointment with the man who had threatened her the day Emmanuel died. His wife was now upon the verge to giving birth and he was equally as impatient to make sure the baby was a boy. He demanded that she conduct the ritual to ensure a boy could be born, but the rule of the universe was that to deliver a boy must be spared; a price that Sabrina chose not to warn him about.

Sabrina lit the idol's candles, illuminating her face as she began to burn the herbs and chant the scripture. The client was standing behind her smiling smugly as she carried out her task, that was until Sabrina looked deeply into his eyes as she chanted who was to be spared in return, matching the smug look on her client's face. The smoke died out as soon as the incantation had stopped.

'So, did it work?'

'It worked' Sabrina said neutrally nodding

As she walked to her next client, she noticed how cold she had become. She had refused to perform the ritual beforehand because she couldn't think of anyone she wanted to swap. She loved everyone in the village dearly but after Emmanuel's death, they meant nothing to her. Now she had to wait until the baby was born and see the client's reaction when his best friend would die in front of him.

Sabrina went to her sister's that night for dinner, the spicy beautiful flavours of the food made Sabrina question why she hadn't eaten before. She kept vomiting every time she ate and the only thing she wanted to eat was, chocolate.

'Sabrina? I thought you weren't eating properly?' her sister asked, noticing that her sister had gained a significant amount of weight in the past few months. Sabrina explained how their mother had complained that her cupboards were bare weeks ago. There was food given by well-wishers still in the freezer.

'I can't keep anything down, so why eat?' Sabrina replied smiling at her sister.

She looked her sister up and down, her stomach looked bloated and her skin glowed but everywhere else Sabrina was skin and bone. She was so thin you could almost hear her bones cracking every time she moved.

'Could you be pregnant?' her sister whispered, Sabrina looked around three months pregnant and Emmanuel died almost two months ago. It made sense.

Sabrina went home after a while, she had suspicions for a while and now her sister had worked it out, she was sure that she was. She wondered whether maybe Emmanuel's death was a sign from the Iwa to start taking better care of herself; to focus more on her family. She cupped her small growing belly as she sat in the kitchen, wondering what to do she smiled and looked at the oxford blue sky.

She decided that this was an opportunity to give new life to Emmanuel; he would be living through the existence of their child. That would have to be enough.

Over the next few months, as her belly grew, the villagers increasingly began to talk. Some believed that the baby was Emmanuel's, but to others it was proof that Sabrina had killed Emmanuel for another man.

'All of a sudden they remember Emmanuel!' Sabrina exclaimed to her mother, she was pacing in the family home; tears of irritation streaming down her face

The man who had begged for a son had started the rumors; he had increasingly lost respect for Sabrina; even though she had performed the ritual. She had a further appointment with the family, their new son had been born and they wanted to see his future. Sabrina had invited the family friends to view the reading too. As she began the reading, she made direct eye contact with the man she had traded for this child, pain had begun surging through his veins and his heart felt cold. He was numb in his right arm and breathing could no longer be taken for granted.

'A baby born in exchange for another person's life is cursed. Your child is broken; he will be sickly and die young. You failed to see that your family savior, the child you should be proud to have is already here. Now you have killed your friend in exchange for a child you have already lost'

The father stared at Sabrina, confused, until he heard the pained groan of his friend and the thud of his dead body hitting the floor. Upon this death, the spell had been locked in and fate could not be changed. Sabrina rose and apologized to the mother and walked out of the home. She was halfway home when she heard loud footsteps thundering after her and her arm being grabbed so hard that she had a bruise for weeks

'Undo it!'

'I warned you, I told you something bad would happen. But you didn't listen to me' Sabrina hissed, her look was hard and dark

The father looked at Sabrina, his lip curling and nostrils flaring. Sabrina recognized the look on the masked individual and his voice transformed her back to that night.

'You killed Emmanuel and the father of my baby; did you really think I'd let you get away with it?'

Sabrina found the knife in the house when she performed the gender ritual, it was large enough to fit the secondary wounds in Emmanuel and it had broken pieces the same size of the pieces found in his body.

'Believe me when I say this Simon, I will find out who else was part of this murder and you will never hear the end of this' Sabrina turned and walked home, watched by the murderer. Simon had been the one to mess up the stabbing, causing someone else to walk in and finish the job. The threat he made was loud and heard by almost everyone. A few hours later the main instigator included Simon in the murder scheme and they watched for the best opportunity to pull off the killing.

When Sabrina arrived home, her body was hot and beads of sweat dripped from her forehead into her eyes making them sting. She poured over books the Oungan had once given her and remembered his warning that people will never really respect a female healer. She found what she was looking for and began the chant, cursing the entire village; that when she died, a disaster would come and destroy the entire village and everyone in it.

With the finishing of the curse, intense pains surrounded her stomach, her back hurt immensely. She struggled in the direction of her bedroom, waiting for the next event to occur. She knew that with the birth of her child, the curse would be placed. It was dangerous for a pregnant woman to place a curse; it would endanger the life of the child and the mother. She had to make sure the baby was born so that the curse could take home.

She struggled through the pain, remembering her experience of delivering other babies. She went through this pregnancy alone and she would end it alone. She always wondered what the pain would feel like and attempted to predict it. She was wrong however; it was worse that she could have imagined. She went through the pain alone and eventually gave birth to a daughter. The baby looked exactly like Sabrina when she was a baby, aside from the eyes. Emmanuel's wide brown eyes now belonged to her daughter, Sabrina thought of Emmanuel wondering if he knew. She thought what if's, about how he would have been during the birth. This did not last long, after the main pain subsided, she filled with the warmth that had been missing ever since Emmanuel's death.

She had her daughter now, another reason to keep fighting for justice for Emmanuel.

'Roseline, I promise you we will get justice for your daddy. Okay? He will be remembered and he will find peace' Sabrina whispered to her baby, kissing her forehead after washing and wrapping her in a blanket

Her cries had been heard by Sabrina's mother and sisters, who raced up into Sabrina's home to see the baby. They lay Sabrina to sleep, watching the baby who cooed as the rest of them cleaned the home

Sabrina's family was complete, and for now that would have to be enough.

CHAPTER 8

Over the next few years, it was more and more confident that the murder of Emmanuel was going to go unsolved. Sabrina had tried and failed to give her statement to the police informing them that she knew who the murderer was. Most of them had subscribed to the theory that she had murdered Emmanuel to be with the father of Roseline, so all her statement would do is prove that she had something to do with the murder.

Under the eyes of the entire village, Sabrina raised Roseline. They would always look for proof that Roseline couldn't possibly have been Emmanuel's, however as she grew up and matured, she looked more and more like her father. Her hair grew darker and curled violently; her arms were long and thin, just like her father. She even had birthmarks that looked eerily similar to the stab wounds Emmanuel received when he was killed. All this did was prove to Sabrina that Emmanuel had returned to her. The Gods were pleased with her for being resilient and gifted her with a reward.

The unusual thing about Roseline is that as she aged, the people of the village began to trust in Sabrina more. The credibility of those who swore they saw Sabrina having an affair had dwindled, and her predictions had become real. Simon's son had died aged two, and his second daughter was talented and thrived. He was now all alone; his wife had gone when their son died and the girls went with her.

The curse was clearly taking place.

By the time Roseline was five, her grandmother had started to see similar behaviour that she saw in Sabrina years earlier.

'She has the gift to Sabrina' she said one day after looking after Roseline while Sabrina had been healing people.

The two observed Roseline over a few months; she would heal a bird that had hurt its wing without any assistance from anyone. Her cousin had fallen ill with a high fever, headache and a sore throat, and without her mother's asking, she cured the illness with a tulsi mixture. This was one of the final pieces of evidence that Sabrina needed to convince herself that Roseline was from the Iwa as a gift. She was a straightforward child, and most of the time, Sabrina would never have noticed; she was there aside from a gentle lullaby, Roseline would sing almost every day.

By the time Roseline was around 10, she was accompanying her mother go to healing rituals and ceremonies. Everyone noticed her calm and focused temperament.

'I am so happy you brought her with you. I remember when the Oungan would bring you when you were young' one old lady smiled as she whispered this to Sabrina after talking to Roseline.

Every day the two would walk hand in hand to their home, talking about their work and what they were planning to do the next day. It was always exciting and fun-filled for Roseline, they avoided some families, but they started to like the village again.

By the time Roseline was sixteen, she was starting to rival Sabrina in her talents. She had built her portfolio of clients that she would perform rituals on and would often travel to the next village in order to help them too. They had become the talk of the village with their talents. Sabrina would proudly talk about her only daughter with her sisters like she had heard them do years beforehand. She finally had stopped looking at herself in the mirror, ignoring the grey hairs that had started to sprout from her head and the awful pain in her stomach that had become a constant issue,

Roseline had also started to ask people about her father, these questions would be avoided, but they still were asked; mostly when she went to treat the police officers. They bowed their heads in shame when they saw her in the village; they had let her down before she was even born, and they all knew that.

Roseline began learning about the threats her mother has been receiving, and with the mention of her father; the cruelty of the village arose again.

'I don't understand why no one will talk about him' she exclaimed on her return home.

'They all know what happened and they don't want to betray whoever it is they are defending" Sabrina replied in her cynical tone, she hated talking about Emmanuel's death. She would frequently tell Roseline about him, how they met and their relationship and how she was after he died; but never his death.

Roseline would journey to the old house, which had decayed due to abandonment. The roof had caved in on itself years before and all features of wildlife had started to make it their home. All that had remained in its original condition was the bathroom where her father died and the room where Sabrina kept her idols. The bathroom was still stained with remnants of his death; the room smelled of stale blood and death.

'Roseline?' her grandmother called; she had followed her into the house after seeing her entering into the village.

'Is this where he died?' she asked while standing in the bathroom.

Her grandmother did not answer. Her face darkened, and her usual happy demeanor had now changed. They stood in silence for a minute or two, observing the bath that stood proudly amongst the rubble.

'Can you please tell me how he died, no one will mention it' Roseline begged, and with the one question her grandmother obliged and told her all she knew about Emmanuel's death.

After they had finished, Roseline and her grandmother walked home and ended the conversation with Sabrina.

'How can we still live here when they killed him?' Roseline asked outraged that she had to grow up and live in the same place as her father's killers.

Sabrina eventually managed to calm her down enough to tell her something she had only just discovered that day.

'You're dying?' Sabrina fell into a chair underneath her upon hearing the news

'I have a growth in my stomach that I cannot cure, I haven't got the strength to go to see a medical doctor, and I don't rightly want to.'

After this revelation, the three women worked on a plan together on what to do. They decided to tell people she was ill and to try to transfer as much work as she could to Roseline like the Oungan had done for her years before.

However, the constant questioning about Emmanuel and the illness had once again restored; the lack of faith felt towards Sabrina. More requirements for Sabrina to perform healings came and they called for Sabrina repeatedly. The hatred towards the villagers had grown again. They had lost faith in her ability to heal as well, so they asked for more rituals. This increased her illness, as the body of a healer goes through a high amount of stress when they perform a ceremony.

'How can they expect you to perform more rituals when you are dying?' Roseline asked one day after her mother returned deep into the night and flailed on her bed.

Roseline had started to blame the village for her mother's illness, she had starved herself for months after Emmanuel's death and still couldn't eat very much, and that was because the village did not even attempt to help her. The village had taken both of Roseline's parents away from her, and no one seemed to care.

She went into her mother's bedroom and stroked her braided hair that had been spread across the bed. After a while, Sabrina fell asleep, holding her stomach that twisted and churned inside her and the only way to ease the pain was to hold it.

The next day, the two were awoken by a heavy banging on the door. Roseline opened the door to an angry woman cradling an arm shouting that Sabrina had not arrived at the house, Roseline looked at the time – 5 am.

'My mother is dying, and you dare to call here at 5 am shouting that she hasn't arrived? She has seen you three times this week and has not charged you for two. If you need help come to me and be prepared to pay, otherwise please come at a better time' Roseline exclaimed slamming the door on the woman's face.

Over the course of the day, both women refused to heal anyone in the village; they had queues of people waiting outside their door, throwing threats at them again. Every time Roseline would walk out of the house to treat another village, she would be greeted with scowls and jibes.

'You'll meet the same end as your father if you're not careful' one villager shouted to her one day.

'Well I thought you didn't know anything about that when I asked you weeks ago' retorted Roseline, unsurprisingly the individual had no reply for that.

When Roseline arrived home, she found her mother unconscious on the floor after attempting to pack her bag to perform rituals on those who were outside the home. Her hair was piled high like Emmanuel's mother once had her hair, and she was dressed in a thin white dress through which you could almost see the mass in her stomach which stuck out of her stomach making her look pregnant again. Her head was heavy and clouded; her mouth ached for water which would cling to her throat when Roseline brought her sustenance.

Rosaline, along with her uncle, dragged Sabrina onto her bed and revived her enough to be able to speak. The water from the flannel on her forehead flowed down her face and provided relief from the warmth in her body.

'This can't go on; we have to punish them. For what they did to dad and what they are doing to you.'

Sabrina smiled and stroked Roseline's face. 'Child, it is taken care of.'

'What do you mean?'

'In Haitian Voudo, the healer is allowed to perform dark rituals as well as healing. That is if a place or person deserves it. The only cost is that they will never see the outcome. The curse comes after the healer's death.'

After explaining this, the two worked together to make sure that the curse would go ahead successfully. Sabrina taught Roseline how to ensure that the curse went through when she needed it to start and explained exactly what the curse would do.

'I need you to make sure that the family isn't in the village, get them to move off the island, I'm not completely sure where the curse will end, but I know it will only hit around this village. So, get them out of here, the curse can only protect three people, so get everyone else out' Sabrina struggled, her chest aching whenever she tried to breathe.

The two shared an embrace, Roseline stroking her mother's hair and Sabrina singing softly in her ear like they had done when she was a child. They thought about their last moments together and comforted each other in knowing that soon Sabrina would be with Emmanuel again. They talked about what Sabrina would have liked their life to be and reminisced about the happy times in their life together.

When finally, they felt that Sabrina's time was coming to an end, they chanted the start of the curse. Locking it in so that they were both sure it would work.

"Hear me now, one day before my death, and when I go, my curse shall unfold. When I enter the ground of my final resting place, I shall take with me the inhabitants of this village who have wronged me and my loved ones shall be protected.'

CHAPTER 9

Sabrina died in her sleep that night; it wasn't painful and disturbing. For once, it was peaceful, her breath and her heart just stopped.

Roseline and Sabrina's mother were there, holding her hand and kissing her fingers lightly.

The sky turned grey as she started to reach her end; many believed a flood was coming and searched for ways to barrier the village before their natural disaster arrived. The clouds gathered around Sabrina's house ready to receive her and guide her to the Iwa.

Roseline watched Sabrina's chest rise and fall, tears soaking her face and intermingling with the oils on her face. She couldn't blink or move; she wanted to see when her mother left. This was the last time she would be with her parents; she needed to take complete advantage of it.

When she finally died, Roseline and her grandmother shed a luxurious tear, gentle but sad. They shook her, thinking maybe she would say one more thing before she left. But Sabrina's work was done, and it was now Roseline's turn.

Her uncle came in after a few minutes and held the two of them for a while

'She's with Emmanuel now. This is a happy day' he said, holding Roseline in his arms as he frequently did when she was upset.

Sabrina's mother and brother then left Roseline to deal with the body. She dressed her in a beautiful white dress and washed her, dousing her with beautiful aromas, so she is ready for burial. She talked to her about her plans for what to do about the curse. Roseline then went out to wait for the body removal people while her grandmother sat with Sabrina's body. For one last time, she sat next to her daughter, stroking and plaiting any locks of hair that Roseline hadn't done correctly. As Roseline sat at the front door, she heard her grandmother singing softly to Sabrina; it was a song she knew well and often heard whenever she was with her grandmother. She longed to listen to the harmonies Sabrina would give with the music. But she knew none would come. Once Sabrina had been taken away to be prepared for her funeral, Roseline examined the home in which she had grown. Remembering every good time, she had with her mother. Packing and remembering she made sure Sabrina was ready to leave. The curse would be soon effective, and she had to make sure all was ready, and everything she still wanted; was safe.

'So, you will stay with me for the next week and then we will go to St Kitts where your uncle is and waiting for your arrival. Okay?' her grandmother whispered as they walked through the village arm in arm carrying Roseline's bags.

Roseline barely slept that night, the thoughts of her mother and the curse raced around in her mind like a carousel as she lay in a new bed with the moon rays gently kissing her face as she tried to sleep. Like her mother when Emmanuel died, Roseline barely ate anything for the next few days and focused on reading and preparing. The house itself was in the process of being prepared to be left and ready for whatever was coming. She made sure to understand how to control the curse and what protective incantations she could create so that the curse could not hit some. She sat by the fire while her grandmother sang and made sure all was in order; Roseline carved out protective charms to give to those she wanted to protect. She copied a symbol that had been drawn into the books for defensive spells and set about making sure all knew about the curse.

She prayed to the Iwa the night before her grandmother left, she knew they would be safe in St Kitts, but she was still afraid. The thought of the curse and her mother made her hyperventilate, and her eyes sting. The next day, she held her grandmother and uncle the last of her family before they clambered on to the final ship to St Kitts before Sabrina's funeral.

They had visited the body a few hours beforehand, knowing they would never be able to visit her. The three of them stood staring at this woman who had not even reached fifty years old yet, but looked older than her mother.

She had been wrapped and embalmed, her coffin had arrived, and the plans had been cemented. They performed the Nine Night Ritual, freeing the soul and allowing it to go to a place of dark water where it could rest.

'Once you deliver the coffin, leave and get as far away from the village as you can. We will bury the body.'

The coffin bearers tried to explain to Roseline that it was their job to bury the body and to make sure it is done correctly.

'I understand, but a lot of people will be at this funeral, and it might break out badly. I don't want you and your workers to be caught up in it' Roseline announced, supported by her uncle who threw some money at them to make them a bit more generous.

Reluctantly, the coffin bearers agreed.

As Roseline watched the last of her family disappear into the distance on their boat, she thought back to the plan. She had two days before the funeral, and still so much work that needed to be done. As she walked back to what remained of her grandmother's home, she inspected the village. She eyed over the mud huts with their intricate designs and allowed the concoction of smells from the marked insult her eyes and her nose. She walked to the raised platform and stood for a moment, breathing in the cool air and feeling the sun rays dance warmly on her face.

'I have done what I have been able to protect my family from you. I am the last of the Debois family in Haiti, and the only reason I am here is to carry out the last of my mother's work. You murdered my father, and the rest of you covered it up. You all had the opportunity to compensate for this, by standing by my mother in her illness. All you did was take further advantage of her, making her illness worse and shortening her life even more. For this, you all are sentenced to die.'

Roseline stood at the podium in silence, glaring at those she knew had wronged her mother and her for that matter. She fingered at her protective idol on her wrist for a moment and then pushed through the crowds in the direction of her home. She was preparing for her final performance in two days' time.

Her books were now en-route to St Kitts with her grandmother, so it was up to her to remember everything.

The day of the funeral came faster than Roseline had anticipated. It was a clear blue day, and the birds were singing in their trees. Roseline said a final prayer to the Iwa, asking for strength with the events that were about to unfurl. She thought about villagers for the first time in a long while, many of them had come to her home begging her to stop the curse, others criticized her for scaring the village for no reason. The nailed coffin arrived at the burial ground next to a pre-dug hole for the coffin to fit inside. They offered to fill in the hole for Roseline, but she knew that nature, in some way, would make sure that the coffin would be taken care of. She started preparations for the funeral, dressing in the healer's clothes as she was to conduct the ceremony. She was so preoccupied with remembering all the scriptures that she barely noticed the crowds arriving at Sabrina's funeral.

Everyone was now here for the funeral,

'Where were all of you when she was alive?' Roseline thought to herself as she eyed everyone of the people who turned up to the funeral.

Simon came, with his head low and guilty. His look was more focused on his son's grave, which was not too far away from Sabrina's final resting place.

'No coffin bearers? They really were poor' some women tittered to themselves before the ceremony began, not realizing Roseline could hear them. Roseline knew, however, that most of them were only at the funeral out of fear. They knew about the curse; she wondered how many would have come if she hadn't have warned them. It would probably have been Roseline on her own with her mother; like it always had been.

Before the ceremony was about to begin, something strange caught her eye. A woman with hair piled high above her head and a beautifully coloured dress on. Her father's mother looked remarkably like this woman; it was as if she was still alive. It couldn't possibly be her; she was so focused on her thoughts about who this could be, that she barely noticed the woman walking towards her with arms open, ready to see her niece.

'Aren't you going to give your Aunt Chantel a kiss?' she smiled as she wrapped her arms around her.

Chantel was taken aback for a moment when she saw her niece, she had the body and the energy of Sabrina, but all she could see in her face was Emmanuel. Her eyes stung with tears that she fought back, some dropped onto the coffin as Chantel bent down to kiss Sabrina's coffin.

'How did you know?'

'Your mother called me the day she died; refused to let me come but she needed me to be there for you as she wouldn't be able to.'

With this reply, Roseline smiled to herself and handed Chantel her idol to protect her against the curse.

'Are you able to make a small adjustment?' Chantel asked before the ceremony could begin

'Emmanuel's murderers are here; make sure they don't die but that they live enough to be in constant pain. I want to know who killed my brother while I still have the chance.'

With that final request, Roseline broke her last protective idol in two and threw it into the air. She knew the Iwa would make sure the murderers would have enough protection not to die, but the curse would still hurt them.

'Will the Iwa be upset that you are performing the ceremony a year early?'

Chantel asked before Roseline began

'They have sent me signs that they are ready for this, her govi broke on its own yesterday. Her soul is prepared to move on.'

Roseline then began the ceremony; she called to the Iwa for protection as her mother returned to their protection. She began chanting and singing, and the congregation sang with her. Solemnly and cynically, they waited for the curse. Some believed that if they went to the funeral, they might be forgiven for everything. But when they saw Chantel arrive, a woman they knew never forgave the village for what they did for their brother; they would not receive forgiveness. It was too late for them to escape; the ceremony had started.

All they could do was to wait for the Iwa to do their work and to hope they would be forgiven.

CHAPTER 10

Once the main rituals had been taken care of, it was time for Sabrina to be placed into the ground. Her pale coffin was light and comfortable for two people to carry. Many volunteered to lower her body, thinking that this would be a final opportunity to save themselves from the curse that was about to hit the village. They prayed to the Iwa for forgiveness and protection and thought in vain of everything they could do to show the Iwa that they were sorry for their actions against Sabrina. Maybe this would have protected them if the Iwa thought for a moment that they meant a word of what they were saying. Her body was placed in the ground, and the men at the front of the funeral proceeded to fill in the hole, they threw flowers and gifts—offerings to their fallen healer in yet another vain attempt to save themselves. Once the ground was flattened over Sabrina's coffin, the sky violently turned grey, clouds began to descend upon the village. Whatever Sabrina had caused was coming, and it was coming soon.

A slab was placed on top of the grave, showing who was lying here. This slab would be the only indication for years to come that Sabrina Debois, the matriarch of the famous healing family, had once lived there. The legend surrounding this curse and her life had made this place a frequently visited relic, many wanted it demolished and rebuilt, but this was a grave to so many people that it seemed disrespectful to do so.

As the curse began to grow, violent winds started to wrap themselves around the people of the village, and the trees began to shake violently, loosening their roots as they were being pulled like magnets towards the cyclone.

'What should we do Rose?' asked her aunt, clutching at her idol.

'Nothing, the Iwa will protect us' she replied looking towards the sky before retreating; saying 'maybe just hold my hand, just to be certain.'

Her hand was cold and shaking when Chantel held it. She knew this girl was brave but somehow to see her slightly anxious relieved her, she was still human despite the cruelty the village put her through. The two of them stood quietly as they noticed clouds circling violently and the winds screaming at the village like a predator running after its prey. It was coming; the two women held each other's hands tightly and continued to look up. For a moment there was a tiny ray of sunshine, which landed on Chantel and Roseline's faces before disappearing again.

'Are you sure that's the curse? It doesn't seem to be coming towards us' Chantel whispered in Roseline's ear.

'That's how I know it's the curse; they never look like they are moving before they hit their target.'

The two of them began to chant neutrally, looking at the village for one last time. They memorized the look of the trees, watched birds frantically fly away from the village and into the distance. As the cyclone grew bigger and louder, the people of the village started to run down the hill, thinking it would protect them from being at lower ground.

The two women stood trying not to look at the cyclone as it drifted closer to them; the screams of the villagers had gotten louder as they had begun to panic. It was not until the hurricane towered grotesquely in front of them, did they for a minute feel frightened. They were sure they would be protected. With a final glance at their village, which was about to be destroyed. The two were whisked away by the cyclone to the other side of Haiti; they would be safe there while the curse did its work on the village.

No one predicted the cyclone; it appeared and disappeared just as suddenly according to weather experts. Relief workers were sent almost immediately to help where they could. When they arrived, however, all that could be found was rubble and dust. The ground was caked thick with mud and sewage as the village had begun to flood after the cyclone had hit; drowning any survivors that were still there.

The marketplace that had always smelled of spices and gorgeous foods was now damp and ruined. Sabrina's old home now looked like a fire pile, the only thing still intact being the bath in which Emmanuel died, filled with water that appeared to be laced with blood. The place in which Roseline was born had crumbled and was whisked away and landed in the village, crushing homes underneath it. The only buildings that remained intact were the two homes of the murderers and the police station. Snakes swam freely in the murky water, infected with tree branches and leaves. Buildings had crashed into one another crumbling them in the process. The entire village was littered heavily with bodies of the villagers; some completely unrecognizable as humans. Animals had managed to get away before the cyclone hit, but something had barricaded everyone into the village. There was no escape and no help for them.

Those in the villages around them recalled how the people screamed to the Iwa for their lives; many people tried desperately to save anyone they could. But again, they were prevented from entering the village. The screams of the people were agonizing, as they watched their certain death looming in front of them. But what the villagers truly hated was the silence, cruel and disturbing; the silence was not something Haiti was used to apart from when something terrible happened.

Aid workers attempted to revive the victims of the cyclone to no avail. Roseline and Chantel lay in the hospital, with slight wounds from when they landed across the island, watching the events unfurl on the news. Numbers of deaths would rise and fall; no one could tell them a straight answer. Some media reporters arrived at the hospital. In some way, they had found out that there had been survivors of the cyclone miles away from it.

Eyewitness accounts had seen them shooting through the air as the cyclone hit, it took a few days for anyone to listen to the accounts. They were ignored and deemed fanciful, but the two women had clothing and symbols respective of the part of Haiti where the village once was; so now everyone knew about them. Roseline received a call from her grandmother after a few days, her voice sounded like smooth caramel; it was comforting to hear her voice again. 'I just can't believe it' cried her grandmother; she had been devastated to see how much damage this cyclone had caused. That village had been her entire life, and she was hurt to see it gone.

'But…it was no longer the village I knew. When I had Sabrina, everyone was kind, but that village was cruel and selfish.

After a few days, two survivors were discovered amongst the rubble. 'They both appeared to have a broken piece of wood in their pocket, which looked like both pieces could fit together. These two people had been on opposite sides of the village. This truly is an unusual case' the reporter said over the news.

With this, Roseline knew that the murderers were to be announced. The news also relayed how everyone else had sadly died in the cyclone. The numbers of deaths weren't absolute as the village did not keep records, but it was assumed that around one hundred and fifty people perished in the cyclone.

Roseline and Chantel were discharged a few days after the cyclone.

Roseline felt as if she was now wholly free to live out her life as she wanted 'You know, you could always come and live with me' Chantel proposed, she lived a happy life with her husband and knew that her church would appreciate someone new to work with them. Roseline did not know what to say about the matter. She wanted to be with her grandmother, but she did not know the way St Kitts worshipped and she wanted to make a better life for herself. Her family needed to evolve and get away from the islands.

The two journeyed to St Kitts that day; they wanted to make sure the family knew they were okay. The cold sea air from the boat stroked Roseline's face, cooling the warmth in her body and soothed the aches on her wounds. They arrived in warm St Kitts to the sound of Roseline's family calling for her in a big jeep that had so many people populated inside it; it was unlikely that Roseline and Chantel would be able to fit in. Sabrina's mother greeted Chantel like an old friend; she had always sent money to Sabrina to help her take care of Roseline and was still there if Sabrina needed rescuing.

'I am so sorry you had to be involved in this' she smiled observing Chantel's wounds and stroking her arms like she had done the night Emmanuel died.

'I feel I paid Emmanuel back for that night by being there for his daughter' she smiled and took another embrace.

The family danced and celebrated Roseline's survival of the cyclone, a plethora of food had been prepared for her and the family was finally happy; able to move on with their lives and try to forget about their awful time in Haiti. The music danced around the streets surrounding her uncle's house and was barely audible from the loud laughter of the family and the jovial shouting. After a few days, it was clear to Roseline that she could not stay in the Caribbean any longer. The warmth and the smells of the island reminded her of Haiti, and she needed to get away from that. Before leaving for America, she conducted a healing ceremony upon the household, making sure the Iwa and her mother would protect them. She left for America with Chantel, eager for her new life; she knew it would be something she would have to get used to. She sat restlessly in her seat on the boat to her new life, watching the Caribbean fade away from her. She said a final goodbye to her mother as they passed Haiti, looking carefully for the remains of her mother's grave.

Years later, Roseline arrived back in Haiti, now married; she wanted to show her husband where she grew up. When she arrived at the village, she was surprised to see that it was completely empty. The rubble of the buildings had been cleared, and nature had taken the village back. Trees had begun to grow again, and grass had started to grow. Roseline climbed up the stone steps that led to her old home. As she looked around where her home once stood, memories of singing with her mother and chasing each other around the house flashed in front of her eyes. Phantoms of her mother and grandmother danced around her.

The murderer of her father had been discovered a week after her arrival in America. Simon had barely survived the cyclone, losing a limb in the process and almost drowning in the flood. He wrote a letter of apology to Roseline, which was thrown in a fire before she could read it.

'He had plenty of time to apologize' she thought, watching the fire devour the letter of false apology.

The final killer, who dealt the cruel blows to Emmanuel, was finally revealed as the police officer who nullified the case and called for it to be disbanded. He had made sure that Chantel would not recognize him by wrapping up as much of his face as he possibly could. He knew when Chantel would be in the station, calling in sick that day. He had been the one to knock on the front door and jump out of the window to escape. He had wanted to kill Emmanuel to torture Sabrina. She had refused continuously to help him become more influential in the village through immoral means.

He had hurt himself badly, but he would live. He called the house regularly, pleading for forgiveness. But none came for him.

He died alone and forgotten, which is precisely what he had been afraid of.

Printed in Great Britain
by Amazon

36485482R00036